Scholastic Canada Ltd.
604 King Street West, Toronto, Ontario M5V 1E1, Canada

Scholastic Inc.
557 Broadway, New York, NY 10012, USA

Scholastic Australia Pty Limited
PO Box 579, Gosford, NSW 2250, Australia

Scholastic New Zealand Limited
Private Bag 94407, Botany, Manukau 2163, New Zealand

Scholastic Children's Books
Euston House, 24 Eversholt Street, London NW1 1DB, UK

Library and Archives Canada Cataloguing in Publication
Larry, H. I.
Night raid / H.I. Larry ; illustrations by Ash Oswald.
(Zac Power)
ISBN 978-1-4431-0254-4
I. Oswald, Ash II. Title. III. Series:°Larry, H. I. Zac Power.
PZ7.L333Ni 2010   j823'.92   C2009-906334-4

Text copyright © 2006 by H.I. Larry.
Illustrations copyright © 2006 by Hardie Grant Egmont.
All rights reserved.
Published in Australia by Hardie Grant Egmont, 2006.
First Canadian edition published 2010.
Illustration by Ash Oswald and Andy Hook.
Design by Ash Oswald.

6 5 4 3 2 1   Printed in Canada 116   10 11 12 13 14

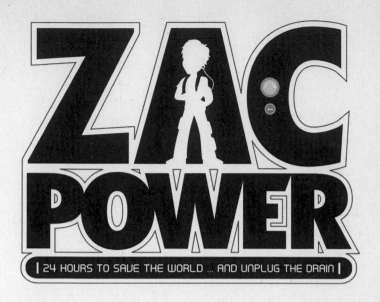

NIGHT RAID

BY H. I. LARRY

ILLUSTRATIONS BY
ANDY HOOK & ASH OSWALD

Scholastic Canada Ltd.
Toronto New York London Auckland Sydney
Mexico City New Delhi Hong Kong Buenos Aires

CHAPTER... ...ONE

It was one of the most embarrassing things that had ever happened to Zac Power. Every morning he caught the train to school and usually his dad dropped him at the station. But today his mum had driven him.

First, she had insisted on walking with him to the platform. Then, right there in front of his friends, she had given him a big, sloppy kiss.

"Have a lovely day, sweetie," she said.

Zac's face went bright red. Behind him he could hear his friends sniggering.

It was at times like this that Zac wished he could reveal his secret identity. Imagine what his friends would think if they knew he was actually a secret agent working for the Government Investigation Bureau (known as GIB). They would be even more surprised to hear that his mum was one too! In fact, everyone in Zac's family was a spy. But this was top secret information. So Zac couldn't say anything.

"And remember," his mum added as she left, "you're helping your dad unplug the drain tonight."

The train tooted.

"Come on, Zac!" yelled his friends, jumping on. But as Zac tried to board he felt a hand on his shoulder.

"Hold it right there!" Zac turned and saw a ticket inspector. "Show me your ticket," she said sternly, flashing her badge.

Zac pulled out his ticket. The inspector looked at it and then shook her head.

"Come with me," she said.

His friends looked worried as the inspector led Zac away. But Zac wasn't worried at all. The badge the inspector had shown him wasn't really an inspector's badge. It was a GIB agent's badge! *Maybe I'm about to be sent on a mission,* thought Zac.

AGENT / MEREDITH DE GARB
SPY NAME / AGENT SHADOW
AGE / 26

SCAN HERE >>>

He didn't always like going on missions. They usually came up right when he was busy doing something fun. But today he had a math test, so he didn't mind at all!

The agent led him to the end of the platform and stood at the top of the escalator.

"I'm Agent Shadow," she said. "Listen carefully – there's no time to waste. You're expected at the GIB Training Centre immediately for a refresher course."

What? Zac was annoyed.

Wasn't the refresher course meant for spies who weren't very good, like Zac's brother Leon? Zac was a good spy. No, Zac was the *best* spy: he was on top of the GIB Spy Ladder every week. Why did he have to go?

Unfortunately, one look at Agent Shadow's face told him that there was no point arguing with her.

"How do I get there?" he asked.

"Down," said Agent Shadow as she shoved Zac onto the escalator. She checked that there was no one around. Then she pulled out a key and turned a lock on the side of the escalator. Instantly the stairs of the escalator folded down and Zac found himself slipping down a giant slide ... straight toward the ground!

Zac quickly reached for his foldable grappling hook and searched for something to secure it to before he hit the ground. But out of the corner of his eye, Zac saw 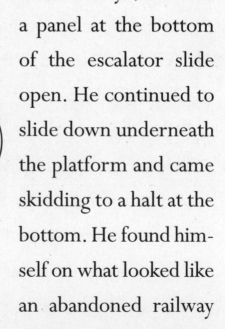 a panel at the bottom of the escalator slide open. He continued to slide down underneath the platform and came skidding to a halt at the bottom. He found himself on what looked like an abandoned railway platform underneath the railway station. *Cool, a secret platform!* thought Zac.

No sooner had he arrived at the bottom than there was a whoosh of air and a shiny, silver train sped out of the tunnel. It stopped right in front of Zac and the doors slid open. Zac stepped onto the train as a voice came on over the loudspeaker.

"Welcome aboard the GIB bullet train, Zac Power," it said. "Next stop: GIB Training Centre."

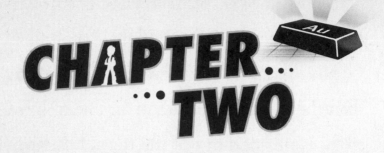

CHAPTER... ...TWO

The train took off at lightning speed. Outside the windows the tunnel walls were a blur. Zac checked his watch.

Surely it wouldn't take long to get to the training centre at this speed? But the train just kept going and going.

Finally, after two hours, the train drew to a stop. The doors opened and Zac walked out to find himself in an office bustling with GIB agents. An agent holding a clipboard came up to greet him.

"I'm Agent Tripwire," he said, handing Zac a padded vest. "Put this on and then go to the simulator down the corridor."

G.I.B. TRAINING VEST
5.7364534kg
>>> UNTESTED

As Zac walked toward the simulator, he wondered what exactly they were simulating that needed such a heavy vest?

The simulator had a strange red glow and Zac soon realized why. Fifty laser beams were sweeping the room!

"Hi!" said a voice beside him.

Zac turned and saw another boy. He was also wearing the training vest.

"I'm Agent Hawk, but my friends call me Ned," he said.

"I'm Zac," said Zac.

"Zac *Power?*" said Ned, looking amazed. "Wow, I can't believe I'm training with you!"

Just then, Agent Tripwire's voice came over the loudspeaker.

"The task is to be the first agent to get through the laser field and reach the other side without getting hit."

"Hang on," said Zac. "I left my Laser Shield in my schoolbag."

GIB agents carried a foldable, lightweight Laser Shield at all times.

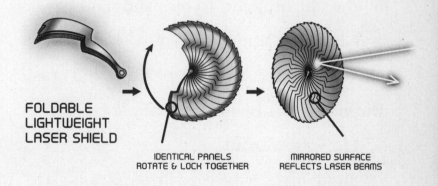

FOLDABLE
LIGHTWEIGHT
LASER SHIELD

IDENTICAL PANELS
ROTATE & LOCK TOGETHER

MIRRORED SURFACE
REFLECTS LASER BEAMS

"No gadgets are allowed in the simulator," replied Agent Tripwire. "You have to rely on your skills."

Fine, thought Zac, *I can do this without any gadgets.*

"Your time starts NOW!" yelled Agent Tripwire.

Expertly, Zac stepped over the first laser beam. The next laser was waist high. Zac leaned backwards and did the limbo below it. Then he dropped to his hands and knees and crawled under the third beam. Zac checked to see how far behind Ned was. But he wasn't behind Zac at all.

He was in front!

Suddenly, Zac heard a buzzing noise. He looked around just in time to see a laser beam swinging toward him. He dived to the ground as the laser zoomed overhead.

Phew! That was close!

But there was no time to rest: three more lasers were heading for him from three different directions.

OK, thought Zac. *There's only one way I'm going to win. I'll have to do a triple somersault over the first laser and then commando roll under the rest.*

It would be tricky. Very tricky. If he somersaulted either a centimetre too high or too low the lasers would get him. It would have to be perfect.

Zac stood up. The lasers came closer and closer, buzzing nastily. But Zac waited until they were almost touching him. Then he leapt into the air and tucked his knees into his chest. One! Two! Three! Zac somersaulted over the top and then dived into a commando roll. He came to a halt and looked up.

Yes! He'd arrived first! But as he stood up, something terrible happened. From nowhere another laser appeared. Before Zac could react it had slashed across his chest.

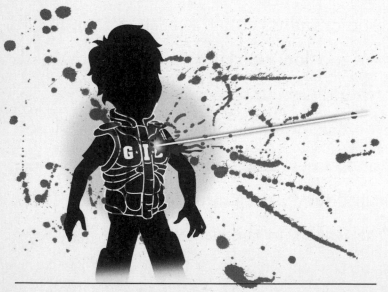

Bright red liquid went gushing all over the place.

"Arrgh!" Zac yelled, as blood spurted all over the room! What was going on? This was just a simulator. Surely he couldn't have really been hurt?

Just then a buzzer sounded and all the lights came on.

"Sorry about the mess," explained Agent Tripwire as he entered the room. "We're trialling a new method where the lasers set off blood packs in the training vests.

To make sure we know who tripped the laser. It still has a few problems though. However, because you were touched by one of the lasers, Zac, you're disqualified. That makes Agent Hawk the winner."

"No way!" said Agent Hawk, in disbelief. "I never thought I'd beat Zac Power!"

"Nice work, Ned," said Zac, putting his hand out to shake Ned's. But Agent Hawk just looked down at Zac's arm. It was dripping with the fake blood that was still oozing out of the training vest.

"Oh yeah, right. I'd better go and change," said Zac as he turned and headed for the locker room.

Just then, both of their SpyPads beeped.

SpyPads are like mini-computers that perform hundreds of functions, including sending and receiving messages from other spies. A spy-mail message had just been sent to all GIB spies, containing the week's Spy Ladder.

Zac didn't bother opening his. He was always on top. But Ned opened his and gasped.

"NO WAY!"

Quickly Zac checked the Spy Ladder. He couldn't believe what he saw either.

Spy Ladder Results, Week 20:

#1 GIB spy: Agent Hawk
          (Ned Hakansson)

#2 GIB spy: Agent Rock Star
          (Zac Power)

#3 GIB spy: Bomber McGee
          (Rik Aston)

CHAPTER... ...THREE

Out in the hall, Zac tried to ignore the funny looks he was getting. He was still dripping fake blood all over the place.

So embarrassing.

Zac made his way to the locker room and was issued with a standard GIB uniform: a hoodie and cargo pants. Luckily his shoes were still OK. Just then another message popped up on his SpyPad.

This time it was addressed just to him.

Zac >>> Go to the vending machine and press E5.

Zac found the vending machine in the corridor and pushed E, then 5. A soft drink bottle fell into the tray. It looked completely normal. Zac unscrewed the top and drank the whole bottle. But there was no mission hidden at the bottom.

Then he noticed something gleaming inside the bottle top. Stuck to the inside of the lid was a flat metal disk.

"Cool!" burped Zac. He needed to get back on top of the Spy Ladder. And going on a mission was the only way he was going to get there.

Zac slotted the disk into his SpyPad.

CLASSIFIED
MISSION RECEIVED 11:00 A.M.

Over the last 48 hours, hundreds of gold ingots have been stolen in night raids on the Brink Bank. Their vault is the highest security vault in the world. Inside the vault are three metal safes. Somehow thieves have emptied two of them. GIB intelligence suggests enemy spy agency BIG is involved and the gold will leave the city in 24 hours. There's no telling what BIG could do with all that gold!

YOUR MISSION
- Discover how the gold is being stolen.
- Catch the thieves.
- Stop the gold from leaving the city.

MISSION EQUIPMENT
Your GIB cargo pants are packed with gadgets. Contact Agent Tech Head for further information.

END

SPY MAIL
>>> DELETE

Agent Tech Head was Zac's brother. Leon wasn't the greatest spy, but he was excellent with technical help.

Zac called him on the SpyPad's satellite phone straight away.

"Hi, Leon," said Zac. "What's the quickest way to the Brink Bank?"

"Catch the underground luge," replied Leon. "It starts from the rear of the training centre. BIG is an *underground organization*, so stay underground as much as possible on this mission." Zac cringed. He couldn't believe that was Leon's idea of a joke! How did he get such a geeky brother?

Behind the training centre Zac found what looked like a toboggan on a hollowed-

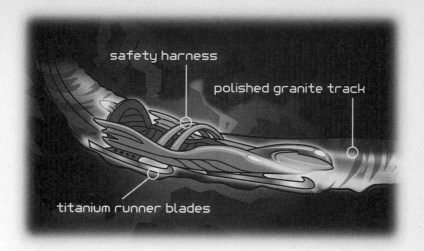

safety harness

polished granite track

titanium runner blades

out track. The moment Zac sat down a metal harness lowered across his chest, forcing him to lie flat.

WHOOSH!

The luge rocketed off. Zac had thought the bullet train was fast. But the luge was much, much faster. It screamed around corners so quickly that Zac thought it might fly off into the air.

Too soon, the ride came to an end as the luge slowed to a stop. Zac got out and looked around. In front of him was a metal door with three security cameras pointing right at him. *This must be the basement entrance of the Brink Bank,* thought Zac. He walked up to the cameras.

"Zac Power, GIB," he said, flashing his badge. Immediately a security guard opened the door.

AGENT / ZAC POWER
SPY NAME / AGENT ROCK STAR
AGE / 12

SCAN HERE >>>

IDENTITY
TOP SECRET

GOVERNMENT
GIB
INVESTIGATION BUREAU

"I'll take you to Mr. Simmonds, the Head of Security," he said.

Mr. Simmonds' office was filled with TV screens monitoring every corner of the bank. Mr. Simmonds himself was sitting at his desk, examining a blueprint.

"I just don't understand how the thieves got in," he moaned. "There's only one door to the vault and it's guarded night and day. Inside it are finely tuned motion sensors which could detect a bug sneezing. Then there are 45 cameras monitoring the outside of the vault 24 hours a day. The gold itself is stored in three separate safes. And the combinations change every day. How could anyone get past all that?"

"I'd better start by watching last night's security video," Zac said.

"Sure," replied Mr. Simmonds, "but believe me, there's nothing to see."

He pressed a button on his desk and one of the screens started playing.

Six hours later Zac had to admit that Mr. Simmonds was right. None of the videos had given him any clues at all. No one had entered the vault and no one had left it. None of the alarms had gone off.

In fact, nothing had happened at all.

"Do you have any idea what time

the gold was stolen?" Zac asked Mr. Simmonds.

"Last night we checked at 9 p.m. and the gold was still there," replied Mr. Simmonds. "But when we checked again at 11 p.m. it was gone."

Zac looked at his watch.

It was almost 9 p.m. now.

"Can you take me to the vault, please?" he said. "Tonight *I'm* keeping watch."

CHAPTER... ...FOUR

The guard took Zac to some stairs at the back of the basement. At the bottom of the stairs was a metal door with a small viewing window. Beside it was a security pad.

"This is the only entrance to the vault," explained the guard. "You can watch through this window. But you won't see anything. Believe me – I've been watching for the past two nights."

I bet I notice things he missed, thought Zac. He was a trained spy, after all!

But by 10:30 p.m. Zac was no longer so sure. The only thing that had happened was that his feet had pins and needles.

I'll just check what the SpyPad says, thought Zac. *Maybe it'll pick up something that the bank's security system has missed.*

He switched the SpyPad to Surveillance mode and pointed it at the door.

Motion Detection: -- 0%.

Sound Waves: -- 0%.

Better check the heat levels too, thought Zac.

If a thief was in there then the heat levels would register around 27°Celsius.

Heat Levels: -- 1064° Celsius

What?

Something very strange was going on.

"We've got to open the safe," Zac said urgently to the guard. "Get Mr. Simmonds down here quickly!"

Mr. Simmonds arrived, looking worried, with the blueprints still clutched tightly in his hand.

"If we've been robbed again we'll be ruined," he said as he disabled the alarms.

And if a robbery has happened right under my nose, thought Zac, *I'll never get back on top of the Spy Ladder.*

The vault door swung open and Zac hurried inside. Everything looked perfectly normal. The third safe was still tightly closed. Zac switched the SpyPad to Heat Detection mode and scanned the safes. The levels seemed normal until Zac pointed the SpyPad at the third safe. Suddenly the temperature jumped up again.

Mr. Simmonds deactivated the motion detectors around the safe. Then he pulled out a remote control and typed a number into it. The safe door sprang open and a wave of heat blasted out.

Zac looked inside and gasped.

It was completely empty!

Mr. Simmonds' shoulders slumped.

"We're ruined!" he moaned.

But Zac wasn't ready to give up just yet. He remembered something his Spy School teacher, Agent Arrow, used to say: *There's always a clue. You just need to look in the right place.*

The safe was too hot to enter, but Zac quickly looked through the pockets of his cargo pants and pulled out a spray can labelled CoolAid. He aimed inside the room and squirted. A jet of freezing air blasted into the room, instantly cooling it.

Zac went inside and looked around.

It looked totally normal.

He bent down and ran his hand across the floor of the safe. It felt rough — as if it was covered in goosebumps. It was also covered with a fine powder.

Better check that out, thought Zac. He activated the SpyPad's Sample Scanner mode and ran the sensor over the powder.

50% Titanium

50% Steel

Zac turned to Mr. Simmonds.

"What's the safe made from?" he asked.

"It's a compound of steel and titanium," said Mr. Simmonds.

So the powder has come from the safe itself! Zac needed a closer look at those bumps. He pulled out his Spyroscope.

The Spyroscope was only the size of Zac's palm but it had a really powerful lens. It magnified things up to 100 times their actual size.

Looking through it, Zac could easily see that the goosebumps were actually the ridges around tiny holes – each one less than a millimetre wide. And there were thousands of them!

But there's no way a gold ingot would fit through those holes, thought Zac, puzzled.

Then Zac suddenly had a thought.

"Can I have a look at that blueprint?" asked Zac. Mr. Simmonds handed it over.

According to the blueprint there was nothing under this level of the bank. But the blueprint was pretty old and crusty. One corner looked like it had been left in

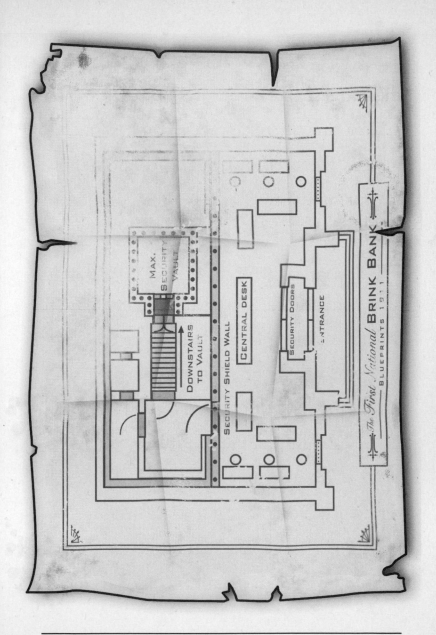

The First National BRINK BANK
BLUEPRINTS 1911

MAX. SECURITY VAULT

DOWNSTAIRS TO VAULT

SECURITY SHIELD WALL

CENTRAL DESK

SECURITY DOORS

ENTRANCE

sunlight and faded. If only Zac had a way of seeing the original drawing.

Then Zac remembered a lesson at school where they'd learned about how blueprints were made before computers were invented. A blueprint was like a rubbing of a grey-lead drawing. There was no way the original drawing would still exist, but maybe there were traces of lead still on the back of this blueprint?

Zac pulled out his SpyPad and switched it to X-ray mode. He ran it over the blueprint and instantly an image flickered onto the screen.

"Look!" said Zac. "There's a tunnel running under the vault."

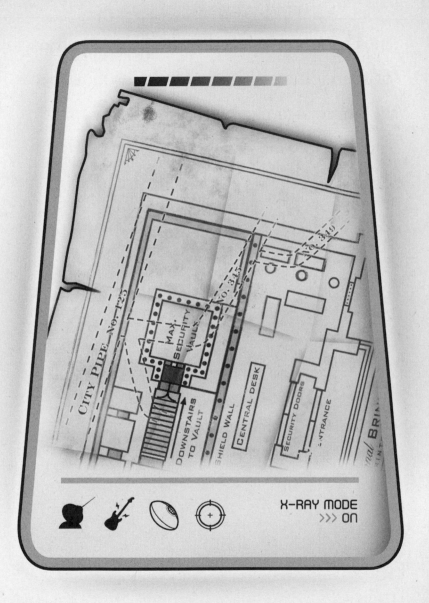

X-RAY MODE
>>> ON

The X-ray showed something else too. Outside the vault was a hidden door that led directly down to the tunnel!

CHAPTER...
...FIVE

Outside the vault, Zac felt along the floor until his hand rested on a hidden lever. Zac pulled it. With a long, groaning noise, a section of the floor swung outwards like a trap-door.

It looked like it hadn't been opened in a hundred years. The thieves couldn't have possibly been using it to steal the gold. Zac had watched more than six hours of security footage and hadn't seen anyone in there.

Just to be sure, Zac scraped up a sample of dust from the side of the trapdoor and ran it through the SpyPad Forensic Tester.

Dust Sample = 95.03 years old.

Well, that cleared that up. There was no way the thieves had used this door.

Zac checked his watch.

Time to get a move on. Zac lowered himself down the hole and landed with a splash in ankle-deep water. Instantly a terrible smell floated up into his nostrils.

It smelled like a thousand rotten egg sand-
wiches wrapped up in wet football socks.

Euggh!

This wasn't any old tunnel … it was a
sewer! Sometimes being a spy was really
gross. No time to be grossed out though.
Zac had to find out where the holes in the
vault led to. Only one problem; it was
completely black.

*Time to check out the rest of my mission
gadgets,* thought Zac.

He typed GADGETS into his SpyPad.
Instantly, a diagram of his cargo pants
appeared on the screen, showing what was
in each pocket. Zac reached into his back
pocket and pulled out a pair of goggles.

When he put them on, the tunnel instantly lit up with a greenish glow.

Night vision goggles. Perfect!

As Zac started wading he heard a squeaking noise. Then something scurried past him. A rat! A big one, too. Zac had a pet rat. But he got the feeling that sewer rats wouldn't be quite as friendly as Cipher.

Before he had any more time to think about it, the goggles picked up something else. Poking up through the ceiling were thousands of very fine tubes.

Zac pulled one out and examined it with the Spyroscope. It was made of a clear plastic. Poking up through the middle was a thin piece of metal. And it was hot!

What was going on? Time to speak with Leon again.

"They sound like the tools used in key-hole surgery," said Leon. "The surgeon makes a tiny cut in the patient and inserts the tubes. The whole operation is then done by pushing tiny tools through the tubes. But I'm not sure how they'd be used to raid a bank."

"I think I know," said Zac. "What does 1064 mean to you, Leon?"

"Oh, that's easy!" said Leon. "That

was the year that Harold, Earl of Wessex was captured by William the Conqueror and forced to swear a sacred oath to him, which then led to the Battle of Hastings and ..."

"Think of something a bit less nerdy, Leon," sighed Zac.

"Well, 1064° Celsius is the temperature gold melts at."

"Exactly!" agreed Zac. "The thieves must have drilled holes in the vault floor to push these tiny tubes through. The wires are then heated to melt the gold and suck the gold back through the tubes — kind of like drinking chocolate milk through a straw. No wonder I couldn't see anyone on the security footage. The thieves were nowhere near the safe while the raid was actually taking place!"

"But you'd need lots of those tubes to steal a safe full of gold in a few hours," said Leon.

"There *are* lots of them," replied Zac. "And if I follow them, they should lead me right to the thieves."

There was no time to lose. Zac hurried along the tunnel, following the tubes.

Gradually the water became deeper and deeper. It wasn't long before it was up to Zac's knees. And it was icy cold!

I need a boat, realized Zac. *But where would I get one?* Then Zac remembered the key-ring his dad had given him for his last birthday. Dangling on the end of it was a tiny body board.

"Umm … thanks, dad," Zac had said. "But isn't this a bit small?"

His dad had winked at him. "If you ever need to use it, just add water."

A body board would definitely come in handy right now, thought Zac.

He unclipped it from the keyring and dropped it in the water. Instantly, it began to expand. Before long it was a full-size body board.

Zac jumped on, grinning.

Awesome!

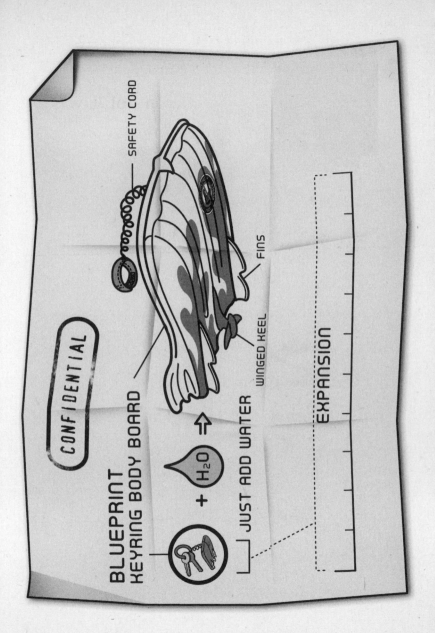

CHAPTER... ...SIX

Zac used his arms to paddle along. It was tiring, but he knew he couldn't take a break or even slow down.

It was already 3:15 a.m.

The gold would leave the city in less than eight hours.

Suddenly a warning message flashed up in his night vision goggles.

ALERT! Life form approaching.

Probably another rat, thought Zac as he continued to paddle. But then two gleaming eyes rose up out of the water and stared at him. Zac's heart pounded. That was no rat … it was an alligator!

I'm out of here! thought Zac. But if he kept paddling the alligator might grab his arm and pull him off his board. Zac *really* didn't want that to happen so he quickly pulled his arms out of the water.

Then he realized he was moving anyway. The current was pulling him down the tunnel!

"Phew," breathed Zac. Hopefully the wires didn't run too much further.

But then Zac noticed something bad. The alligator was following him! And it was getting closer by the second. Then it disappeared underwater.

Uh oh, thought Zac. He remembered something he'd seen on Leon's favourite nature show, *Creepy Creatures*:

When an alligator disappears under your boat, LOOK OUT! It's planning to tip you over!

CREEPY CREATURES

A moment later Zac felt something bumping underneath his board.

Zac slipped but managed to hold on to the board. Then the alligator attacked again. This time it hit the board so hard that Zac found himself somersaulting off the board and into the water.

He turned to see the alligator swimming toward him with its jaws wide open. He tried to scramble back onto his board again – but he was covered in the gross sewer water and kept slipping off.

The alligator lunged for him. Zac did the only thing he could and held up the board in front of him.

SNAP!

The alligator's jaws clamped down hard on the board. But to Zac's surprise they bounced right open again.

And, even stranger, there weren't tooth marks on his board! Then Zac noticed a sticker near the base:

That was good, but Zac had something new to worry about. Right in front of him the tunnel divided into two. Above the right-hand tunnel was a big warning sign.

DANGER! DO NOT ENTER!

But the wires that Zac was following led off to the right.

The thieves probably put the sign there to stop anyone from following the wires, Zac thought to himself.

Still holding his body board between him and the alligator, Zac angled himself to go down the right-hand tunnel. As soon as he did, the alligator stopped swimming.

Another sign appeared on the roof.

TURN BACK NOW!

Then, to Zac's amazement, the alligator turned and swam away! What was in this tunnel that could even scare an alligator?

Zac felt a pang of fear. But as long as he was following the wires and getting away from the alligator he had to keep going.

Zac finally managed to scrabble back onto the board. He was being sucked down the tunnel pretty fast now. He almost didn't

SERIOUSLY,
YOU DON'T WANT TO
GO DOWN THERE!

see the last sign as he sped past:

But there was nothing he could do about it now, even if he wanted to!

Beneath the body board the water churned and bubbled. Rocks jutted up and the current tried to drag Zac under. There was a noise, too, growing louder and louder. It sounded like there was an enormous washing machine up ahead.

Zac grasped the board tight as he swooshed around a bend. And then Zac saw what was making the noise.

White water rapids!

Zac held on tight as he entered the rapids. He'd been in white water before, but these rapids were about Class 6 — really strong and *really* fast. First the water flung him to the left. Then it threw him to the right. The disgusting sewer water splashed into his face, covering his goggles. Luckily he managed to wipe them clear just in time to see that he was heading straight for an outcrop of jagged rocks!

Whoa! Zac managed to steer around them. Then he grinned. *This is actually pretty cool.*

Skilfully he began swooshing around each obstacle and dodging the snags. The longer the rapids went, the better Zac got. When the waves were breaking just right, Zac even managed to pull a cool 360° flip off the sewer wall! In fact, he was almost disappointed when the rapids died down and the water level dropped.

Eventually the water was so shallow that Zac had to climb off the board. He started following the wires down the tunnel, but didn't get very far. Up ahead the tunnel was completely bricked over, and the wires disappeared into a crack in the ceiling.

He'd reached a dead end!

CHAPTER... ...SEVEN

Zac checked the time.

He had looked the wall up and down but there was no way he could follow the wires any further. It looked like he was stuck. And then something else his teacher Agent Arrow used to say popped into his head: *When one trail comes to an end, find the start of the next one.*

OK, thought Zac, *if I can't go over it, then maybe I'll have to go under it.* He looked down for some sort of way to get past the wall and suddenly saw something shining.

A chocolate bar wrapper!

He picked it up and looked at it closely. On the back of the wrapper was written *Made at Bigmouth Chocolate Factory.*

It was a bit of a long shot, but Zac had nothing else to go on. He pulled out his SpyPad and entered "Bigmouth Chocolate Factory" into the Location Finder.

A set of coordinates flashed up on the screen. *No way!* The factory was right above him! Quickly, he looked for the closest manhole in the roof so he could get out of the sewer. He could see a crack of light up above him, but there wasn't a ladder on the wall to help him reach it.

Zac unclipped his collapsible grappling hook from his belt. He swung it into the air and snared it on a brick near the hole. Then he climbed up the rope.

When he got to the roof, Zac pushed

open the manhole a crack and looked out into a long hallway. At the end was the strangest looking door Zac had ever seen. It was shaped like a mouth with two rows of gleaming teeth.

This has to be the Bigmouth Chocolate Factory! It wasn't a very friendly looking door. In fact Zac got the feeling that visitors weren't really welcome.

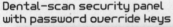

Dental-scan security panel with password override keys

Then Zac heard a noise. There were people approaching. He managed to close the manhole just as they walked overhead. Once they'd passed, he opened it again to look out and saw two people in Bigmouth uniforms.

"I'm tired of working so hard," grumbled one of them. "When is this job going to finish?"

"The trucks are arriving at 11 to collect the load," replied the other worker.

Zac's brain started ticking. *I bet they're talking about the gold,* he thought. *I've GOT to get into that factory!*

One of the Bigmouth workers went up to a small screen beside the door and opened her mouth. There was a flash of light and then the giant set of teeth parted to let them through.

It's doing a dental scan for security, realized Zac. After the workers had passed through, the doors came crunching together. *I don't want to find out what happens if you fail*, Zac thought to himself.

Zac snuck up to the screen. He had just the thing to get past this door … the GIB regulation sports mouthguard! It was made of a highly reflective plastic developed in the GIB lab. *That should confuse the dental scanner and override the door's security*. Zac slipped the mouthguard on and smiled into the screen.

There was a flash, and Zac waited nervously. *Yes!* Slowly, the mouth-door opened and Zac quickly jumped through.

But then something terrible happened. The laces on his right runner got caught between the teeth on the mouth door — like floss between teeth.

Zac *hated* flossing his teeth but not as much as he was going to hate getting his leg bitten off by this door!

Zac tugged at his foot. This was bad. He was going to have to take off his shoe to get free. He started fumbling with the laces.

Why hadn't he bought the Velcro shoes!

Then the door started beeping. The

teeth were closing and were going to do some major damage if he didn't get out of there quickly! He gave one last tug of his leg and then felt himself falling flat onto his face. He was free!

Unfortunately his shoe was now on the wrong side of the mouth, which had firmly closed. It was his favourite pair of runners too. He'd saved up his pocket money for months to buy them! But there was nothing Zac could do except kick off his other shoe and hope no one found it.

He had more important things to worry about ... like how he was going to explore this place without getting caught.

CHAPTER... EIGHT

Zac hid behind a door and called Leon.

"I'm in the Bigmouth Chocolate Factory," he whispered. "I need a disguise. Fast!"

"Check the pocket of your hoodie," replied Leon.

Zac checked and found something that looked like one of his mum's stockings.

"It's a battery-powered Chameleon Suit," explained Leon. "It's made up of millions

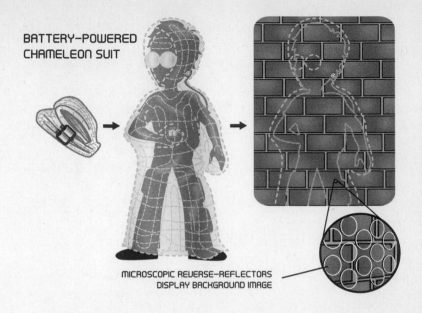

BATTERY-POWERED
CHAMELEON SUIT

MICROSCOPIC REVERSE-REFLECTORS
DISPLAY BACKGROUND IMAGE

of tiny reverse-reflectors that automatically blend in with the surroundings."

Zac heard footsteps approaching.

Time to see if this thing works, he thought, slipping on the suit and flipping the switch to ON. It covered him entirely — even his face — but was thin enough to see through.

Zac held his breath as a Bigmouth worker brushed past him. *Phew! The suit must be working!*

Now that he was disguised, Zac felt safe to look around. But which way should he go? The factory was like a maze, with paths going off in all directions.

Then, in the distance, Zac heard a voice booming over a loudspeaker:

"7:12 A.M. LESS THAN FOUR HOURS TO GO. WORK FASTER!"

Zac made his way down the winding corridors, following the voice:

"7:15 A.M. LESS THAN FOUR HOURS TO GO. WORK FASTER!"

The voice sounded like a robot.

It's an electronic message, realized Zac.

He turned a corner and found himself at the entrance to a huge factory floor. Hundreds of people in Bigmouth uniforms were busily making chocolates.

Zac started snooping around. In the first room there were huge vats of liquid chocolate. The chocolate was being pumped along thick pipes into a second room. The door to the second room was locked, but there was a conveyor belt leading out of this room which had chocolate bars on it.

In the third room Zac found a giant wheel rolling out sheets of foil. There was probably enough foil in the room to wrap the whole factory. Another machine was wrapping the chocolate bars in foil at lightning speed, then stacking them into boxes. There must have been at least 500 boxes in this room alone.

Zac thought for a second.

The only part of the process he couldn't see was happening in the second room. What was going inside the chocolate bars? Maybe the gold is hidden inside the chocolate! That would explain why the door to that room was locked and why everyone was working so hard.

Zac grabbed a chocolate bar from the conveyor belt. It was heavier than a normal chocolate bar, but not as heavy as pure gold. Maybe they'd mixed the gold with another alloy to make it lighter?

Still hiding beneath his Chameleon Suit, Zac peeled back the foil on the chocolate bar. Then he took a bite. Sure enough, there was something hard inside the bar. And when Zac looked at where he'd bitten he could see yellow gleaming through!

But something was wrong. The yellow stuff wasn't shiny like gold. And it tasted sweet. *It's honeycomb!* realized Zac.

So where was the gold?

Disappointed, Zac ate the rest of the chocolate bar and then scrunched the wrapper into a ball to put in his pocket – he didn't want to leave any clues behind.

But then he stopped.

Hang on. Isn't foil usually silver?

This foil was gold. It was also very, very shiny. Zac grabbed the SpyPad and quickly checked the foil with the Forensic Tester.

The results flashed up on screen.

100% Au.

Au is the chemical symbol for gold! thought Zac triumphantly. *They're disguising the gold as foil and wrapping it around chocolate bars!*

A plan this devious could only be the work of one organization ... BIG!

But if this whole operation was run by BIG then all these Bigmouth workers must be *enemy agents!*

And that meant Zac was outnumbered by about 500 to 1.

I'm going to need some help, realized Zac.

Quickly, he sent a message to Leon:

BACKUP REQUIRED

SEND GIB AGENTS
TO BIGMOUTH FACTORY ASAP

Now I'd better go somewhere safe to wait, thought Zac. But as he stood up a hand clamped down on his shoulder.

"Going somewhere?" sneered a voice.

Zac looked up. Uh-oh … He was completely surrounded by BIG agents. But how could they see him with the

Chameleon Suit on?

And then he noticed a small label sewn into the seam of the Chameleon Suit.

WARNING! CHAMELEON SUIT BATTERIES ONLY LAST FOR 60 MINUTES!

"You must be Zac Power," he said. "We've been expecting you. In fact, we've even prepared somewhere for you to stay."

He turned to the worker on Zac's left and said, "Take him to The Cage!"

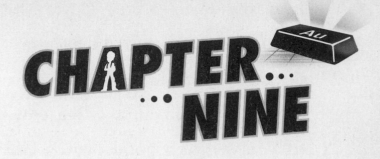

CHAPTER... ...NINE

The two BIG agents led Zac down the winding corridors of the factory. Zac was a black belt in judo and it would have been easy for him to get away. But he didn't even try.

GIB know where I am and this could be a chance to get more information about this operation. Zac decided to use an old favourite spying trick: flattery.

"This whole plan is very clever," he said. One of the agents grinned at him.

"Yeah, that's because BIG agents are much smarter than you dumb GIB agents."

"I bet you've got a good plan if GIB decides to search the Bigmouth factory?" said Zac, trying to look impressed.

"Of course," boasted the other agent, "Up in the Bigmouth factory they really *are* making chocolate bars — if someone is clever enough to find us down here under-neath the factory, then we'll just open up the roof and escape in BIG helicopters."

So Leon wasn't joking when he said that BIG is an underground organization! thought Zac.

Unfortunately Zac didn't have time to

find out anything more before they reached The Cage.

One of the agents patted Zac down.

"He's got hundreds of gadgets in his pockets!" said one of the agents as she pulled gadget after gadget out of Zac's cargos: his grappling hook, Laser Shield, Tramp-o-Socks, even his iPod!

"We don't have time for this," snarled the other agent. "Take your cargo pants off, Zac Power. We're not going to have you using any of your high-tech gadgets to escape – but you can keep your iPod, I guess. What harm can that do?"

The door in front of Zac slid open to reveal … a very normal looking room.

"Go on," growled one of the agents, pushing him in the back.

How high tech, thought Zac as he walked into the middle of the room. Then one of the agents pushed a button near the door. Instantly, dozens of laser beams shot out from the walls surrounding Zac – he was in a laser beam cage!

"See ya later," laughed the agents. "We've got some chocolate to finish wrapping."

The door clanged shut.

Zac looked at his watch.

This wasn't the first time he'd been stuck on a mission wearing only his underwear, but he had no idea how he was going to get out! *I can't even get out of a simulator without getting hit,* he thought. *And this time the blood wouldn't be fake!*

Even if he could dodge the lasers there was still the problem of getting past the locked door with his pants and his gadgets on the other side. He couldn't just hope that the GIB backup would work out that BIG was *underneath* the Bigmouth factory. He had to find a way to alert GIB. He had to open the BIG factory roof!

He switched on his iPod and started flicking through the extra features.

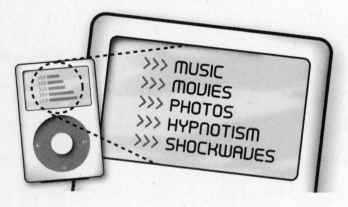

>>> MUSIC
>>> MOVIES
>>> PHOTOS
>>> HYPNOTISM
>>> SHOCKWAVES

There was nothing he could use!

Zac ran his fingers through his hair, thinking hard. His hair felt messy.

He turned over the iPod to check his reflection in the back, but then Zac forgot all about his hair. He'd just had a brilliant idea! The back of a GIB issued iPod was made of mirror-like material.

Zac carefully slid the iPod mirror into the path of one of the laser beams. Instantly the laser beamed back onto the wall.

Just as he'd hoped! The mirror was acting like a Laser Shield. Where the laser was reflecting onto the wall a hole began burning. Zac angled the mirror so that the laser beam hit the lock on the door. The smell of melting metal filled the air.

Then ... **CLANK!**

The door creaked open.

Next he moved the mirror so that one laser sliced across all the others. The beams buzzed and glowed angrily for a moment, then ... **POW!**

They exploded in a shower of red sparks, like fireworks. *Cool!*

Zac ran over to where his cargo pants lay crumpled on the ground. He pulled them on, then checked the time.

He only had 33 minutes to stop the gold from leaving the factory!

CHAPTER ... TEN

Stealthily, Zac crept back to the factory. If he got caught again he would fail this mission. Then BIG would have heaps of money to do evil things with. And, most importantly, Zac would never get back on top of the Spy Ladder!

By the time he reached the factory door it was already 10:33 a.m.

Zac stopped. He couldn't just walk in

without his Chameleon Suit, but somehow he had to get in without being seen.

Zac looked around. Above the factory door was an air-conditioning pipe covered by a grille. *That pipe must go right over the factory floor,* realized Zac.

Quickly Zac swung his grappling hook up and pulled the grille off the vent. Then he scrambled up into the pipe.

There was just enough room for Zac to wriggle down the pipe on his belly. He crawled along until he came to another grille he could look through.

Below him BIG agents were scurrying around frantically. *I have to open the emergency roof exit,* thought Zac. *Then the GIB agents* in the Bigmouth factory above will realize that BIG are actually underground.

The loudspeaker's electronic voice boomed right next to Zac's ear:

"WORK HARDER! DEPARTURE TIME IS 20 MINUTES AND COUNTING."

Zac frowned. It was hard to think while that voice was blaring.

Zac looked through the grille again. No wonder the voice was loud. The speaker was directly below him! On top of it was a small box with the word CONTROLS printed on the front.

Hang on, thought Zac. *Maybe I could reprogram the loudspeaker!*

It was worth a try. Very carefully he

pushed the grille aside so there was a gap large enough to put his hand through.

I hope no one looks up, thought Zac. But everyone was working far too hard to notice him.

Zac lifted the lid on the control box. Inside he found a miniature keyboard, a jumble of cables and a control panel.

Zac paused. *I could really use Leon's help with this,* he thought.

Leon was an expert hacker. But there was no time to call. Zac was going to have to do it himself.

There was a red wire and a purple wire attached to the control panel. Zac knew they'd studied this at Spy School.

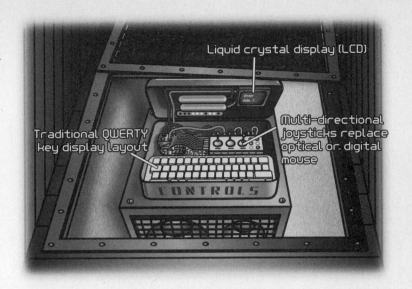

Liquid crystal display (LCD)

Traditional QWERTY key display layout

Multi-directional joysticks replace optical or digital mouse

CONTROLS

If he unplugged the correct wire it would disconnect the speakers and he'd have time to reprogram the controls. But if he unplugged the wrong one the alarm would go off!

The computerized countdown boomed out on the loudspeaker again:

"TEN MINUTES TO DEPARTURE!"

Zac's forehead began sweating.

Which cable?

Zac squeezed his eyes shut and imagined himself back at Spy School. He pictured the classroom and the other students. Then he imagined his teacher, Agent Arrow, at the front of the room.

"Whatever you do," he remembered him saying, "don't unplug the purple wire."

Zac opened his eyes.

That was it! He grabbed the red wire and yanked it out.

Then he waited.

Was the machine going to explode?

A second passed. Then another. The alarm was flashing up on the control panel but there was nothing coming out of the speakers! *All right!* Zac grinned and began reprogramming the controls.

Once Zac had finished typing in a new message he carefully touched the two ends of the broken wire together and the speaker spluttered into life. Then the same bossy voice filled the air.

But now it was saying Zac's words:

"ATTENTION BIG AGENTS! GIB AGENTS HAVE DISCOVERED THE UNDERGROUND LAIR. GO TO PLAN B! BIG HELICOPTERS ARE WAITING TO FLY YOU TO SAFETY. OPEN THE ROOF IMMEDIATELY!"

Zac waited.

Would the BIG agents fall for it?

"Hurry! Open the roof!" yelled some-one. There was a loud, screeching noise that sounded like hundreds of fingernails being dragged down a blackboard.

A second later the factory was flooded with light. It took Zac a moment to realize what it was. *Sunlight!* The BIG agents all looked up as the gap widened.

"Hey, there aren't any helicopters!" shouted someone, angrily. "Close the roof, it must be a trick!"

Oh no, thought Zac. The screeching began again as the roof started closing.

Zac was racking his brain with a plan to stall BIG. All of a sudden, dozens of ropes were flung over the edge of the hole. And a second later a GIB agent zoomed down each rope!

"What's going on?" yelled the BIG agents as they were surrounded.

Zac heard a familiar voice below him.

"What's going on is that your plan has been foiled by the best GIB agent around ... Zac Power!" Agent Tripwire from the GIB Training Centre was looking up at Zac and smiling.

"Nice work, Zac," he said as GIB started arresting the BIG agents. "It's safe to say you'll be back on top of the Spy Ladder next week. Do you want to come down from there and we'll go grab a burger to celebrate?"

"Er, thanks," Zac said politely. "But I have something else to do."

"Oh?" said Agent Tripwire, "Another mission already?"

Zac smiled as he thought of his dad waiting at home for him to help unplug the drain.

"Kind of ..." he said.

... **THE END** ...